THE RUNAWAY SKELETON

BY KATHLEEN M. MULDOON
ILLUSTRATED BY PHILLIP HILLIKER

Librarian Reviewer
Marci Peschke
Librarian, Dallas Independent School District
MA Education Reading Specialist, Stephen F. Austin State University
Learning Resources Endorsement, Texas Women's University

Reading Consultant
Elizabeth Stedem
Educator/Consultant, Colorado Springs, CO
MA in Elementary Education, University of Denver, CO

STONE ARCH BOOKS
www.stonearchbooks.com

Vortex Books are published by Stone Arch Books
151 Good Counsel Drive, P.O. Box 669
Mankato, Minnesota 56002
www.stonearchbooks.com

Library of Congress Cataloging-in-Publication Data
Muldoon, Kathleen M.
    The Runaway Skeleton / by Kathleen M. Muldoon; illustrated
by Phillip Hilliker.
        p. cm. — (Vortex Books)
        ISBN 978-1-4342-0800-2 (library binding)
        ISBN 978-1-4342-0896-5 (pbk.)
        [1. Foster home care—Fiction. 2. Apache Indians—Fiction.
3. Indians of North America—Southwest, New—Fiction. 4. Mystery
and detective stories.] I. Hilliker, Phillip, ill. II. Title.
PZ7.M889Ru 2009
[Fic]—dc22   2008007980

Summary: Brothers Topo and Mono discover a skeleton in a shack
and decide to play detective.

Art Director: Heather Kindseth
Graphic Designer: Kay Fraser

Photo Credits
Capstone Publishers/Karon Dubke, all (except for barn door)
Stone Arch Book/Kay Fraser, barn door

1 2 3 4 5 6 13 12 11 10 09 08

Printed in the United States of America

TABLE OF CONTENTS

CHAPTER 1
Bones 5

CHAPTER 2
Spooky Neighbors 13

CHAPTER 3
Eagle's Nest 20

CHAPTER 4
High-Tech Detectives 27

CHAPTER 5
On Luther's Land 35

CHAPTER 6
Death of a Hunch 44

CHAPTER 7
Acorn Stew, Peridot, and Luck 55

CHAPTER 8
Skeleton Hunt 64

CHAPTER 9
Big Bad Wolf 73

CHAPTER 10
Underground 82

CHAPTER 11
Lucky Lizard 92

CHAPTER 12
A Great Team 100

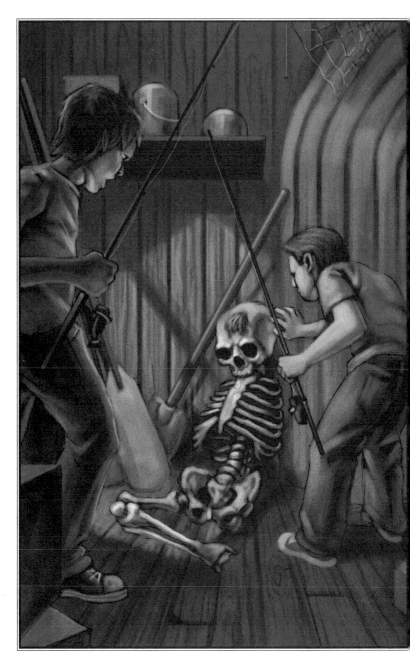

[CHAPTER 1]

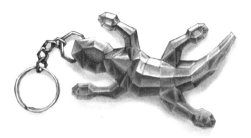

BONES

We only broke into the shed because of the storm. My brother, Mono, and I had planned to go fishing at the creek, that's all. Just have fun and catch some fish.

Then the lightning came. I grabbed my brother and we headed quickly for the first place we saw.

That was the shed. I had to push out a window to get inside. And that's where we found the skeleton.

You'd think an eight-year-old kid would be scared, but Mono wasn't. I guess he's seen too much TV.

"Cool!" Mono said. "Hey, Topo, where do you think this guy came from?"

I gulped. I've seen bones on TV, but not like this.

The skeleton was missing both its arms, one leg, and all its teeth. A patch of dark hair stuck to the skull. It lay in a heap next to an old rowboat. It was gross.

"How should I know?" I said. I tried to sound normal. I didn't want to scare my little brother, but we were in big trouble. We'd only lived in Eagle's Nest for one week. Now we'd broken into a place and found a skeleton. Could there be any bigger trouble than that?

"We should call 911," Mono said.

"Are you loco?" I screeched.

Mono frowned. "No, I'm not crazy," he said.

"How can we explain to the cops what we're doing in here?" I asked.

We'd been to the creek just once before, with Mr. Barker. He and his wife, Ellen, were our new foster parents.

Mr. Barker wanted us to call him George, but I couldn't. Not yet.

Usually I only stayed in a foster family a few weeks. Then they would decide that having a teenager around was too much. But the Barkers had taken Mono and me. I wanted it to work for Mono. He needed a family.

I looked through the window I'd removed. I could barely see the Barkers' house. The creek wound through woods beyond the end of their ranch. Mr. Barker said it ran into the Colorado River.

I put my hand on Mono's shoulder. "I'm sorry I yelled," I said. "But think about it. The cops find two kids in a place they're not supposed to be, with a skeleton. We might end up in jail!"

Mono frowned. "It's just bones, Topo," he said. "The guy must've been dead for years. Maybe even a hundred years."

I sighed. Mono had a point.

Still, something told me that it wasn't time to tell anyone about our discovery. At least not yet.

"Do you want to be a detective?" I asked Mono. "It would have to be our secret, just the two of us. We can find out who owns this place. Maybe we can even find out who this guy was. Maybe it's not even a guy!"

Mono's dark eyes sparkled. He jumped around, doing his funny little dance.

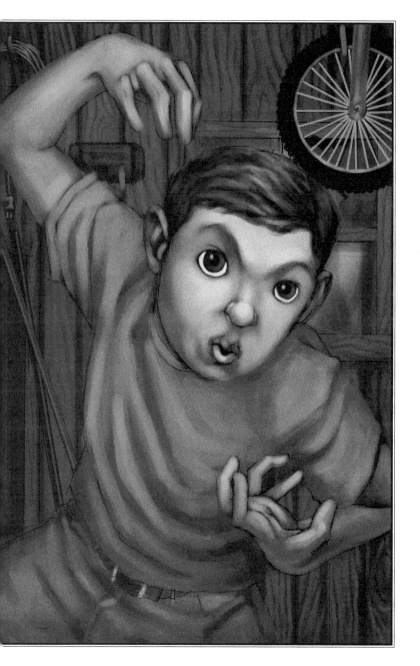

That's why I call him Mono. It means "monkey" in Spanish.

"Yeah!" he squealed. "Topo, if we solve this mystery, will the Barkers want to keep us? They seem pretty cool. Ellen sure is a great cook!"

Only Mono would think of his stomach at a time like this. He was right, though. So far, the Barkers had treated us well.

Mono was four and I was ten when Mom and Dad went to Mexico and left us with our grandmother. They never came back. When Grandma died, we had no family left.

Mono and I had each been in eight foster homes, but we'd never been together. Until now, four years later. The Barkers might be our last hope, at least until our parents came back.

If they ever did.

I pushed open the rusty shed door. The rain had stopped. The air smelled like clean sheets. Sunlight peeked out from behind a cloud.

I turned and knelt down beside the skeleton. I'd never touched human bones before. I ran my finger over a rib. It felt smooth and cold. Then I noticed something.

"Spiders built webs all over the rowboat," I said. "But there are none over the skeleton."

"So it hasn't been here that long!" Mono said.

I knew right then that Mono would make a great assistant. I would need to work on keeping him quiet around the Barkers, though. When he's excited about something, he'll blab it to the whole world.

"Come on," I said. "Let's fix this window and get out of here. It's almost time for dinner."

With Mono's help, I put in the glass I'd pushed out. We put a little mud around the glass to hold it in. Before I shut the door, I took one last look at the heap of bones. Then we jogged up the dirt path that led to the Barkers' house.

[CHAPTER 2]

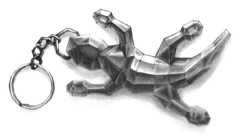

Spooky Neighbors

Mrs. Barker put a huge plate of barbecued ribs in front of me. Mono had his eyes closed as he sucked the tasty meat off the bones. He looked like he was in barbecue heaven.

"So, Hector, what were you two up to today?" Mr. Barker asked me.

Just like I couldn't call him "George," Mr. Barker couldn't get used to calling me by my nickname, Topo. Hector is my real name. Mono's real name is Alex.

"Uh, we just messed around," I said. I stirred my mashed potatoes. "We went down to that creek you showed us. To fish."

"We caught a catfish," Mono added. "But Topo said it was too small, so we let it go." He looked like a clown with red sauce smeared around his mouth.

Mrs. Barker dipped the corner of her napkin in her water glass. Then she reached over and cleaned my little brother's face.

"Well, then, I guess there are no fish for me to clean tonight," she said. "Did you get caught in the rain? I thought of you boys as I drove home from work. I was afraid you'd be out when that storm roared through."

She looked right at Mono for an answer. I wanted to kick him to remind him of our secret, but Mr. Barker's legs were in my way. So I just held my breath.

(15)

"We found a tree and got under it," Mono said. Then he looked right at me. He seemed proud of himself for coming up with a good lie so quickly.

Mr. Barker frowned. "Trees aren't the best places to take shelter when there's lightning," he told us. "It's best to get indoors."

"Actually," I said quickly, "we found some old buildings and got close to them. Kind of across the creek."

I wanted Mr. Barker to know we were safe. I didn't want him to think I couldn't take care of Mono. Or myself. "Please pass the potatoes," I added.

Mrs. Barker handed me the potatoes. Then she turned to her husband. "They must have been on Luther Mueller's property. Doesn't his land go up to the creek there on the northern edge?"

Mr. Barker shook his head. "No," he said. "But some buildings that Luther built are on public land near the creek."

Mr. Barker was an archaeologist. He was also a teacher at the college. He studied old stuff that he and his students from the college dug up around town.

Mr. Barker did most of his digging on a nearby reservation. He always knew what was going on there and in the town of Eagle's Nest.

So the shed we'd been in belonged to Luther Mueller. I needed to know more about him. What kind of guy was he?

Was he the kind of guy who would get mad if he found out that two kids broke into his shed? The kind of guy who would dump someone's bones like garbage?

Suddenly, I wasn't hungry anymore. But I needed more information.

"Mr. Barker, does Luther Mueller have kids?" I asked. "I mean, he lives so close and all. I thought maybe Mono — I mean Alex — and I can hang out with his kids."

"He does have a son," Mr. Barker replied. "His name is Wolf. It's hard to guess his age because he's big like his father. I haven't seen him around lately. And I know that Luther has been out of town."

"Does he go out of town a lot?" I asked, trying to act like I didn't really care.

"Yes," Mr. Barker replied. "Sometimes they're both gone for weeks at a time. They're not very friendly," he added, shaking his head. "They're almost secretive, with all the brush blocking their house. It's really just an old cabin. I've never seen a woman there, so I don't know if he's divorced, a widower, or what."

"I heard that his wife left him a while back," Mrs. Barker added. "We've only lived here a few years. I never met her. Funny, isn't it? Small town like this, everyone knows everyone else. But no one seems to know the Muellers. They've lived here a long time, too. I think that's strange."

Yeah, strange, I thought. Strange that the boy, Wolf, had disappeared. Suddenly my stomach felt like someone had punched it. Could the bones in the shed be Luther Mueller's son?

I looked across the table at my brother. Detective Mono was practically asleep in his chocolate pudding. I'd have to wait until morning to share my plan with him.

Tomorrow, while the Barkers were at work, Mono and I would get some answers. It was time we met the townspeople, up close and personal.

CHAPTER 3

EAGLE'S NEST

I had only been to Main Street in Eagle's Nest one time. Mono and I had gone to the store with Mrs. Barker.

I liked the small downtown. It was different than the big city I was used to. Main Street in Eagle's Nest had a drug store, a post office, a library, and a gas station. In the second block were a bakery, a grocery store, and a pizza place. At the very end of the street, there was a movie theater.

I decided I needed to visit Main Street. I needed to talk to some people, and there weren't any close to the Barkers' ranch.

"Is it all right if I take Mono into town?" I asked Mr. Barker at the breakfast table the next morning. Mrs. Barker had already left for work.

Mr. Barker took off his glasses and cleaned them with his napkin. "Sure," he said. "Would you like me to drop you off? I'm going to the college this morning."

The college where Mr. Barker taught was about an hour's drive away. Mono looked at me. I knew he wanted to ride in the truck. But I wanted to walk. I needed time to plan.

"We'll walk," I said.

Mr. Barker stood and reached in his pocket. He took out two five-dollar bills and handed one to each of us.

"You can't go into town without some spending money," he said. "The drug store has a lunch counter."

"Hey, thanks!" Mono said.

As we walked down the dusty road toward town, I tried not to look at the shed. Mono skipped along next to me.

"This isn't a fun trip, you know," I told him. "We've got to find out who those bones used to be."

"Well, that doesn't mean we can't buy some neat stuff," Mono said. "Besides, you can't walk up to someone and ask them if they're missing a skeleton."

Mono was right. This wasn't going to be easy.

I stopped and put on my most serious face. "Mono, those bones were a person!" I said. "We need to find out who that person was."

"I know," Mono said quietly.

"I've thought about this," I told him. "Maybe Mr. Barker will help us, but not until we know what's going on. We have to prove we had nothing to do with the bones. Got it?"

Mono folded his arms. "Of course I get it," he said. "Do you think I'm loco? I dreamed about those bones last night. I dreamed they were chasing me. But I don't want to think about skeletons all day long!"

I grinned. After all, he was just a kid. "I'll give you time off for fun," I promised. "Right now, we've got to try to find someone to talk to. We need to find out about Luther Mueller's son, Wolf."

Mono sighed. "Okay," he said. "But those guys are out of town anyway. They might never find out that we broke into their shed. Now can we eat?"

I smiled. Mono always takes care of his stomach.

As we headed toward the drug store, I thought about what Mono had said. He was right. It could happen that no one would ever realize we'd been inside the shed.

Did that mean we should just pretend we'd never been there? Did that mean we should forget about the bones?

At the drug store, I sat at the counter and ordered a double cheeseburger. I knew that I couldn't just forget about the skeleton. I'd seen stuff on TV about fingerprints and evidence. That didn't make me feel any better.

Sooner or later, someone would find the skeleton. Sooner or later, they would find out that Mono and I had been with that skeleton. That meant that I needed to solve the mystery soon.

After I ate my burger and washed it down with a chocolate shake, I took a small notebook from my pocket.

As Mono slurped the rest of his soda, I added to the notes I'd written last night:

Who is the skeleton in the shed and how did it get there?

Possibilities: If no one's seen him, the skeleton might be Wolf Mueller.

Did Luther Mueller kill his son?

Did LM kill Wolf and then leave town?

WHY?

CHAPTER 4

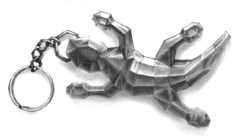

HIGH-TECH DETECTIVES

After lunch, Mono and I went to the library. I had to buy him a candy bar to get him to come to the library instead of going to a movie.

The library looked like a building from an old cowboy show. It was small and built from rock. Stone lions guarded each side of the main door. On the way inside, Mono stuck his arm in the face of one of them.

The librarian reminded me of the librarian at the last school I went to.

This one's name was Miss Phinney. She had kind-looking eyes behind her glasses.

"Hello, boys," she said in a soft voice. "Are you here for the Tree House Adventure?"

"What's that?" Mono asked.

"A man is here from the zoo in Desert Canyon," she said. "He's showing a film, and he brought some reptiles. He's in the room behind the children's books."

"Cool!" Mono said. "Can we go?"

"You go," I said. I couldn't believe my luck. That ought to keep Mono busy while I work, I thought. I had some serious questions that I figured only a librarian could answer.

Mono raced off to the Tree House Adventure. After he closed the door behind him, I smiled at Miss Phinney.

"What can I help you with?" she asked.

"Can you help me find books about how police find out things from fingerprints and stuff?" I asked.

"Ah," Miss Phinney said, "I think I can help you. Let's start by taking a look online. By the way, do you live in Eagle's Nest? I don't think I've seen you before. Do you have a library card?"

When I told her we were living with the Barkers, she smiled. "Of course!" she said. "Professor Barker mentioned that you boys would be here for the summer. I'll get library cards for you and your brother. Then I'll sign you up for the computer. You can find out just about anything using the computer."

Soon I had a purple library card and my very own password to use the computers. Miss Phinney showed me how to search for stuff. Then she left me alone.

I knew one word that I needed. "Evidence." So that was the first thing I typed into the search window on the computer when I sat down.

Wow! Hundreds of possibilities popped up on the screen. Miss Phinney came over and helped me narrow it down.

By the time I'd finished, I'd filled a whole page with notes. The main thing I'd learned was that I couldn't figure out who the skeleton was by myself. Only a detective with special tools could do that.

But that didn't mean I was out of luck. I could get some information. Maybe I could get enough clues to show Mr. Barker.

Mono finally came out of the Tree House Adventure room about half an hour later. He was hopping up and down. He looked really excited.

"Do you think Mr. Barker would let me get a lizard, Topo?" he asked. "They're so cool! Mr. Solis said we can catch some right near our house. I could keep it in a jar with holes in the lid. Then I could catch insects and worms and stuff to feed it."

"Maybe," I said. "But Mrs. Barker might not like lizards in the house. You could ask her. First we've got work to do." We headed out of the library.

"You won't believe all the stuff I found on the computer," I said once we were outside. "The most important thing is that we've got to go back to the shed. We've got to measure the skeleton."

Mono looked at me like I was an alien. "No way, Topo," he said. "Let's just leave it alone. No one's come after us. That Mueller guy is gone."

"They could still figure out we broke in," I told him.

Mono shook his head. "We're only staying with the Barkers for the summer. We'll be at some other house by the time anyone finds that skeleton. No one will even remember we were in this town." He looked kind of sad when he said that.

I didn't know what to say. Mono went on, "Please, Topo, let's just have fun the rest of the summer. Catching lizards and stuff."

I was tempted to go along with my little brother. Maybe no one would go in the Muellers' shed.

But a voice in my head kept telling me that danger was ahead.

I felt in my bones that I needed to find out who that skeleton was. And I needed to do it soon.

I put my arm around my little brother. We began the long hike back to the Barkers' ranch.

"We'll do fun stuff," I promised. "But you are my best helper, Mono. Tomorrow morning we'll go to that shed, measure the skeleton, and look for a few other clues I learned about. It could all be over after that."

"I hope so," Mono grumbled.

I saw storm clouds gathering on the horizon. I had a feeling that they were only the beginning of trouble.

CHAPTER 5

ON LUTHER'S LAND

The next morning, I was full of ideas. Instead of sleeping, I had begun to solve the mystery of the skeleton. At least in my mind. Now all I had to do was prove it. Before Mono got out of bed, I filled several more pages of my notebook.

It was Saturday. In the afternoon, the Barkers were taking Mono and me to show us the Apache reservation. There was a special market on Saturdays. That left Mono and me all morning to explore.

It didn't take long to feed the chickens and lead the Barkers' two horses to the pasture. Those were our only chores.

Soon we headed toward the creek. I explained to Mono that we were going to explore Luther Mueller's house before we went to the shed.

Mono stopped. "What?" he yelled. "This is getting too creepy. Let's go to the shed, measure those old bones, and get out of there. Forever."

I decided it was time to explain my ideas to Mono. "The bones have to be Wolf or Luther Mueller," I said. "That's the only thing that makes sense. One of them killed the other one. Whoever did it left town. Mr. Barker said that both of them are big. We might not be able to tell whose skeleton it is, but we'll know it's one of them if it turns out to be tall. Like over six feet tall."

Mono scratched his head. "So how come we're going to the house? What good will that do? The skeleton's in the shed."

"Trust me," I said. I knew I sounded lame. "We might find some clues, that's all." I didn't want to tell him that I just had a feeling.

Thorn bushes and rotting trees lined both sides of the dirt driveway that led to the Muellers' house.

There wasn't a gate or a nice fence. Just paper signs tacked on trees. The signs read "Keep Out."

When we came to the clearing where the cabin stood, I gasped. An old pickup truck was parked in front. A bright painting of a fish covered the driver's side door.

"Someone's here," I whispered.

"Well, duh," my brother said. "Now can we get out of here?"

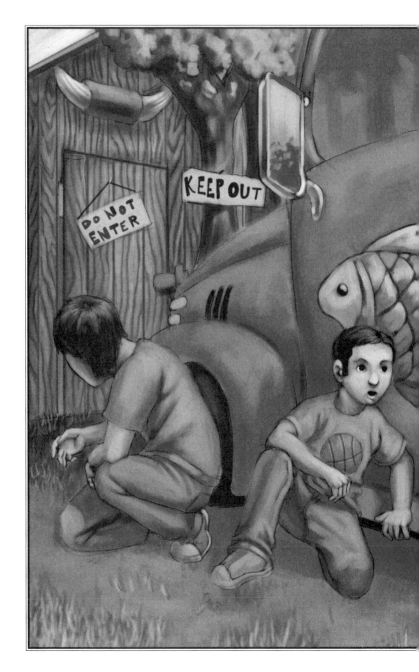

We ducked behind the truck. I still had a good view of the cabin. No curtains hung in the windows. The front door stood partly open.

To the right of the house was a small building surrounded by barbed wire. I guessed that it was a dog kennel. I didn't see or hear any dogs, but I sure didn't want to get close enough to find out if there were any.

I looked to my left. The woods surrounding the clearing would allow us to creep pretty close to the other side of the cabin. I motioned for Mono to follow me.

Dried leaves crunched under our feet. Low branches slapped our faces as we crept through the brush. Soon we were on the left side of the cabin under a slightly opened window.

I was surprised to hear voices coming from inside.

"Do you think there are gangsters in there?" Mono whispered.

I stood up as much as I dared and put my ear to the wall. Then I heard: "SUFFERING SUCCOTASH!"

"What is that?" Mono whispered nervously.

I turned to him. "Daffy Duck," I told him.

Mono's eyes opened wide. "The gangsters are watching cartoons?" he asked.

As silently as I could, I backed away from the cabin. Then I ran back into the woods. Mono followed me. I didn't stop until we were safe.

"I think Wolf is in the house," I said. My detective brain was on full power. "I don't think Luther Mueller would watch kid shows."

"Is Wolf old enough to drive?" Mono asked. "The truck was there."

That was a good point. "I don't know," I said. "I guess he must be."

I didn't want to waste time thinking about it. We needed to see that skeleton. Right away.

I didn't have to convince Mono. He was already racing back toward the creek. I followed him. We saw some patches of newly dug dirt as we ran. I wanted to stop and explore those, but we didn't have time.

At first, the shed looked exactly the same. But as we got closer, something didn't look right.

At first, I wasn't sure what it was. I couldn't tell what was different. The window we'd put back was still in place.

Then I realized that the door was slightly open. I knew that Mono and I had pulled it shut behind us the day of the storm. My stomach leaped into my throat.

"Maybe the wind blew the door open," Mono whispered.

I shook my head. I didn't think so. "Follow me," I whispered to Mono.

We had to find out if anyone was there. And if anyone was listening, they had to think it was our first time at the shed. So, speaking loudly, I said, "Hey, Mono, look! An old shed. I wonder who owns it. Let's peek inside and see what it is."

We waited. No one came out from the shed. I was pretty sure no one was inside.

"All right, Topo," Mono yelled, looking proud that he'd figured out what I was doing. "I don't think anyone will mind if we just look."

"That's enough," I said, lowering my voice. "No one's in there. Come on, let's just measure the skeleton and get out of here."

The door groaned as I pulled it open all the way and stepped inside. It took a minute for my eyes to adjust to the dark room.

Once we were inside, I could tell that someone had been there. A few things were different in the room.

For instance, I was pretty sure someone had moved the rowboat. And I was definitely sure of something else. The skeleton was gone.

CHAPTER 6

DEATH OF A HUNCH

"It's gone!" I said stupidly.

Mono looked excited. "I knew it!" he said. "Skeletons can't run away. That means there never was a skeleton. Don't you get it, Topo? We just dreamed it."

I snorted. "How can two people dream the same thing?" I asked, rolling my eyes at my brother.

"They just can," Mono said.

"You're loco," I told him.

"Not as loco as you thinking a skeleton can run away," Mono said. "Now can we get out of here?"

"Can you wait just a minute?" I said impatiently. "I know the skeleton didn't run away. Someone took it. Or moved it. I need to look for clues. Help me move this rowboat."

The boat was heavier than it looked. We managed to drag it about six inches. In the dim light, I could make out the edge of a trap door beneath it.

Wait a second. Had someone buried the skeleton under the shed?

Just then, I felt something. I looked down at the biggest rat I ever saw. It ran over my shoe.

I don't know which of us ran outside faster — me, the rat, or Mono. The rat disappeared in the tall grasses.

"Gross!" Mono gasped, jumping up and down. "Come on, Topo. The only things living in that shed are rats."

"I don't care about rats," I said. "There's some kind of door under the boat. I saw the hinges. I don't think our skeleton ever left that shed. I think someone buried it underneath. You know what? I bet there is a secret passage under there."

"Where does it go?" Mono asked.

That was a good question. Maybe a tunnel connected the shed to Luther Mueller's cabin. But why?

I didn't have everything figured out. Not yet. But my hunch said that I was going to figure it out, soon. I just didn't know how.

A whistle on the other side of the creek made both of us jump. It was Mr. Barker. He was walking toward us.

"You fellows about ready to go?" Mr. Barker said. "Ellen decided that we'll wait to eat lunch until we get to the reservation. She wants you to try a special Apache food, acorn stew."

"Ew," Mono said. "We're going to eat those green acorns that squirrels eat?"

Mr. Barker laughed. "Not exactly, Alex," he said. "The cook grinds acorns into a sweet flour. Then they make a stew. The acorn flour makes the stew nice and thick. I think you'll like it."

"Maybe," Mono replied. He was usually willing to try anything once. "What else are we going to do?" he asked, hopping down the trail next to Mr. Barker.

"You boys are in for a treat," Mr. Barker said. "There's a special peridot show at the Cultural Center."

"What's 'pair of dots'?" Mono asked.

"Not dots," I said. "Peridot. It's a stone, kind of green. They make jewelry and stuff with it."

What I didn't say was that I remembered it because our mother was born in August. The peridot was her birthstone.

Mom wore a sparkling peridot on a chain around her neck. Dad had given it to her on her birthday one year.

"That's right, Hector," Mr. Barker said. "The San Carlos Apaches have the largest peridot mining business in the United States."

"What do the Apaches do with the stuff, whatever it's called?" Mono asked.

Mr. Barker smiled at him and said, "They mine the rock by hand, and then make it into all kinds of things, especially jewelry, like your brother said."

"I don't get it," Mono said. "What's the big deal about it?"

"You never get it!" I teased him.

In his teacher voice, Mr. Barker said, "They believe that owning a peridot will bring you peace and good luck."

The Barkers' house was only a short walk away. We all piled into Mrs. Barker's van for the trip to the reservation.

During the ride, Mono chatted happily with the Barkers. They taught him all about the San Carlos Apaches. I tried to listen, but I kept thinking about the door in the shed. Where did it lead? What was hidden under it?

"Digging would have disturbed the Indian burial grounds," Mr. Barker was saying. "That's why the town decided not to build another road near Luther Mueller's land when he asked for one."

"Because it would have gone over graves?" Mono asked.

"Right," Mr. Barker said, nodding. "So right now, this main road is the only way we can get to the reservation from our part of the county."

"Is there a cemetery by the creek? I didn't see any graves," Mono said.

Mr. Barker shook his head. "There is a burial ground on the reservation," he said. "But before the reservation existed, the Apache buried their dead wherever they could. So it's possible there are graves throughout town."

That got my attention. Graves throughout town? Maybe that meant skeletons could be all over town too.

"How come Mr. Mueller wanted a road anyway?" Mono asked.

"Probably so he could poach more easily," Mrs. Barker said. I could tell from her voice that she did not like Luther Mueller.

"What does poaching mean?" Mono asked. "Is it something bad?"

Mrs. Barker sighed. "Poaching means hunting without a license," she explained. "It's illegal. Hunters need to get permission in order to hunt. More than once, Luther was caught hunting without a license on reservation land."

"Some of the finest fishing and hunting in the state can be done on Apache land," Mr. Barker added. "They are generous about letting people hunt there. They let people do it as long as they get permission first, and pay a fee. So poaching on that land is not only illegal, but bad manners, too."

"I get it," Mono said quietly.

When we reached the reservation, a woman with dangling earrings and a long yellow dress greeted us at the entrance.

Mr. Barker paid the fee for all of us. Then a kid about my age waved us over to a field where we could park.

It took ten more minutes to walk back to the buildings we'd passed.

Suddenly I stopped. I recognized one of the parked vehicles. Someone was opening the door, which had a fish painted on it.

It was the truck we'd seen at the Muellers' cabin.

Mr. Barker recognized it too. "There's Luther Mueller," he said. "Looks like his boy's with him, too."

Sure enough, an enormous, blond, bearded man stepped out from the driver's side of the truck.

At the same time, a younger guy got out from the passenger side. They both went inside a restaurant.

Mono and I looked at each other. I knew just what Mono was thinking, because I was thinking the same thing.

So much for my hunches! Luther and Wolf Mueller were very much alive.

CHAPTER 7

ACORN STEW, PERIDOT, AND LUCK

I had plenty of time to study the Muellers, because Mr. Barker led us to the same restaurant. I had a good view of both father and son from our table.

As I drank iced tea, I watched Luther Mueller shovel spoonfuls of food into his bearded face.

Wolf had blond hair like his father, but no beard. He looked a couple of years older than me.

He was big, though. His arm was about as big around as my waist. I didn't want to mess with him. Or his father.

A waitress placed steaming bowls of acorn stew in front of us. It tasted as good as it smelled. Soon I was mopping up the few remaining bits with a piece of sweet brown bread.

"Man, this is good stuff," Mono said. "I never knew an acorn could taste so good."

"Want more?" asked Mrs. Barker. "Or would you rather have dessert? They've got great fry bread. It comes with butter and chocolate."

The fry bread was fantastic. I was so busy eating it that I didn't notice when the Muellers left. When the waitress came with the check, I glanced over and saw that the two men were gone.

Going to the peridot show was like being on a planet filled with green glass. Long tables were covered with the shiny yellow-green crystals, made into all kinds of stuff.

Mrs. Barker went right to a jewelry booth. She tried on several silver bracelets, each with at least one peridot.

Mr. Barker, Mono, and I walked up and down the aisles. At one table, he showed us the way peridot looks when it comes out of the mine. I could barely see the green inside the ordinary gray rock.

Mr. Barker explained that the green part had to be removed and polished. He held up a finished peridot. It shined like green ice.

On the next table were statues, boxes, lamps, and vases decorated with the shiny gems. One table even had dog and cat collars made with peridot.

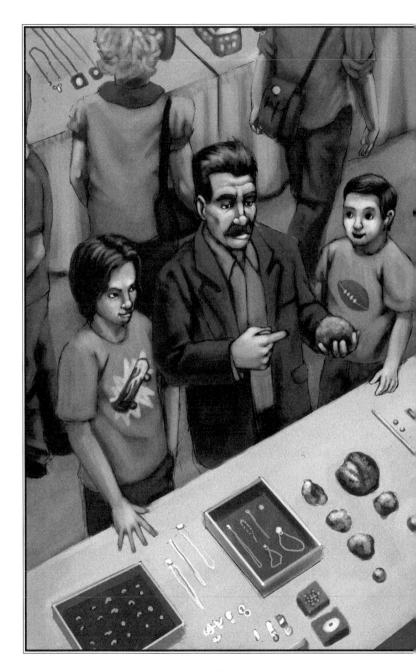

Mr. Barker led us to another booth. There, he told Mono and me to pick out something for ourselves.

"If you want good luck, this is the place to find it," he joked.

I touched wallets, belts, and vests, all studded with peridot. Then I spied a silver keychain with a peridot lizard attached.

The little lizard felt smooth as ice and would fit in my pocket. It was the coolest thing I'd ever seen.

"I like this," I said, holding it out to Mr. Barker.

Mono was already wearing a straw hat with a peridot band. He looked like a cowboy.

Mr. Barker picked out a belt buckle for himself. After he paid for our treasures, I put the keychain in my jeans pocket.

Now, I know this sounds weird, but that peridot lizard really did make me feel lucky. As we walked around the rest of the building, I felt stronger. Taller.

I decided there had to be some Apache magic in those shiny green stones.

On the way back to the car, we stopped and watched a dance. I loved the lively drum beats and colorful costumes. As I tapped my toe to the beat, everything in the whole world seemed good.

Mrs. Barker put one arm around cowboy Mono and her other hand on my shoulder. Her new bracelets jingled.

"So, boys, how do you like the reservation?" she asked.

"Cool!" Mono exclaimed.

"It's awesome," I said.

We didn't see the Muellers again. I wondered if they'd gone back to their cabin. I pictured them watching cartoons. I almost laughed out loud.

As we left the reservation, we saw a group of people near the exit. They held up signs toward people leaving in cars. The signs read, "Protect our land!" and "Our burial grounds are sacred."

Mrs. Barker waved to them as we passed. She was a nurse on the reservation, so she knew a lot of the people.

"Do you know what that's all about?" Mr. Barker asked her.

Mrs. Barker nodded. "From what I've heard, someone's been digging near the mines," she explained.

"Are they after the peridot?" asked Mr. Barker.

"I guess," Mrs. Barker said. "And that's bad enough. But mostly the people don't want any graves disturbed."

I thought about the freshly dug spots I'd seen that morning. The ones near the shed where the skeleton had been, and then not been.

Mr. Mueller's property wasn't on the reservation. But Mr. Barker had said some graves were probably near the ranches, where the county had decided not to build a road.

I closed my eyes and thought about that. I ran my fingers over the peridot keychain in my pocket. A fuzzy picture began to form in my mind.

By the time we pulled into the Barkers' driveway, I was pretty sure I knew who the skeleton was. I also thought I knew how it got into the Muellers' shed.

And I was pretty sure of another thing. The Muellers were involved in something much worse than a bunch of bones.

I, Topo Garza, wanted to prove it. Before I went to bed, I wrote everything down in my notebook.

Then I put my lizard keychain on top of it. Just for luck.

CHAPTER 8

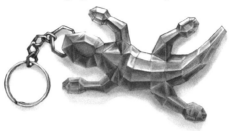

SKELETON HUNT

The next morning Mr. Barker invited Mono and me to go to one of his digs. He and his students were digging in Desert Canyon. They were looking for buried stuff from the Mexican War, back in 1846.

"Awesome!" Mono said, scarfing down his last pancake. "Can we go, Topo?"

I smiled as I rubbed my peridot keychain. Last night I'd decided that it would be too dangerous to have my little brother along on the skeleton hunt.

Mr. Barker's invitation gave me a way out. I guess my lucky keychain worked!

"I'd like to go fishing," I said. "Would you mind if I stayed here?"

"I think you've earned a day to yourself," Mr. Barker said. "Ellen's packed us great lunches. Hector, why don't you take yours down to the creek? Look's like it's just you and me, Alex."

Mono did his monkey dance. "I'm ready!" he said happily.

The house was quiet after they left. I hadn't been alone since we'd come to the Barkers' house.

I tried to stop worrying as I got ready to leave for the shed. Everything would be okay. This was my only chance to make sure my hunches were right before I asked Mr. Barker for help. I needed to take that chance.

I stuck the lunch Mrs. Barker had made in my duffel bag, along with a screwdriver from Mr. Barker's workbench. Then I went to the garage and found the little spade Mrs. Barker used in her garden. I put that in my bag too. It might come in handy.

I decided to leave my notebook on the nightstand. I didn't need it. Every word I'd written in it burned in my memory.

Then I made sure my lucky keychain was in my pocket. In my other pocket, I put a small flashlight and a pocket knife. I was ready to face anything.

My first stop was the Mueller cabin. As soon as I came to the clearing, I breathed a sigh of relief. The truck was gone. Yes!

I gave my lucky keychain a victory pat. Then, just to be sure, I tiptoed to the window and listened. No cartoons were playing inside.

It was time to find the runaway skeleton.

I knew the bones hadn't really run away. In fact, I was pretty sure that the skeleton was old. I guessed it was one of the Apaches who'd fallen in battle over a hundred years ago. It all seemed to fit.

My theory was that while Mr. Mueller had been messing around the peridot mines, he'd dug up the skeleton.

He didn't want to get caught, so he threw the bones in his truck. He had planned to bury them later. He put them in his shed and forgot about them for a while.

I was certain that one of those freshly dug areas I'd seen the day before now held the missing skeleton.

It took me a while to find the first spot. Someone had dragged old brush over the newly dug soil, so the spot was hidden.

I quickly started moving all the branches away. Soon I had cleared off the soil rectangle I'd seen yesterday. With Mrs. Barker's spade, I shoveled off the top layer.

Clunk! I hit something hard. I shivered. I imagined the toothless skull, grinning up at me.

But it wasn't bones. It was a wooden box. With the screwdriver, I pried off one corner. It was filled with gray rocks.

I knew right away what the rocks were. We had seen the same thing the day before at the reservation. The rocks were all unfinished peridot!

I stood and kicked dirt back over the box. Then I carefully put the branches back.

There was another freshly dug area nearby. I was pretty sure there was a box of peridot buried there too.

That could only mean one thing. The skeleton was in the shed. And I had a feeling it was under the trap door.

I raced to the shed. It looked exactly the same as how Mono and I had left it the day before.

Inside, I swung my flashlight around to every corner. I noticed one thing I hadn't seen before. Stacked against a wall were shovels and an ax.

They were all dirty, like they'd been used recently. I thought Luther probably used them to get the illegal peridot.

The rowboat still blocked the trap door. Without Mono, I couldn't move it.

I sat on it and thought. Did I really have to find the skeleton? Since it wasn't a murder victim, I could just let Mr. Barker know about it. He would take care of it.

But I couldn't turn off my detective brain. I wanted to find out what Luther was doing with the peridot.

Was he selling it? Could that explain their trips out of town?

I rubbed my lucky lizard keychain again. Suddenly, it was like the peridot lizard shouted an answer in my ear.

The kennel! The Muellers didn't have a dog. But the kennel by their house was surrounded by a barbed-wire fence. I needed to see what was in the little building.

"Thanks, Lizard," I said to my keychain.

I headed back to the clearing. It was still empty. I hid my duffel bag in a patch of brush.

Then I found a place where the barbed wire was rusted. One solid kick broke it and I scrambled under the fence.

Finally, I found a door on the side of the little building. The door was locked. I used my screwdriver to pry it open.

Inside the room, I saw a workbench and piles of paper and boxes.

Suddenly a hand grabbed my shoulder. I whirled around and slammed into the chest of Wolf Mueller.

CHAPTER 9

BIG BAD WOLF

"What are you doing in here?" Wolf asked. His hot breath blew through my hair.

I gulped. "I, uh, I was out hunting," I began.

Wolf grabbed a handful of my shirt. His hand was as big as a football. He backed me into a wooden counter that wrapped around three of the four walls. From the corner of my eye, I saw the glare of a computer screen on the counter.

"Hunting? Don't you mean snooping?" Wolf snarled.

Hey, Lizard, I thought. *I can't reach you right now, but if ever I needed luck, it's now.* But no wise words flooded my brain.

I'd have to outsmart Wolf. I put on my friendliest voice. "I'm sorry," I said. "I'm new around here and I just saw this place. I thought it was abandoned."

"So you just go around and break into abandoned buildings, huh?" Wolf said angrily. "You don't even think that someone might own them?"

I tried to smile. "Well," I said, "no, I don't break into buildings, usually. I guess my curiosity got the best of me. I'll just leave you alone to do whatever it is you were doing. I'm sure Professor Barker will be looking for me. I'm staying with him for the summer."

Wolf laughed meanly. "I know who you are," he told me. "My old man told me there were foster kids staying at the Barkers' ranch. Then we saw you staring at us in the cafe. I don't like anyone looking at me. Neither does Pa."

With a final push, he let go of my shirt. I slumped against the wall.

Wolf looked around, as if trying to find a spot to put me. Or bury me.

He picked up some scissors. My hand went up to protect my throat. But Wolf backed over to a giant spool of twine on the far end of the counter.

He cut off two pieces. Each one was about as long as my arm. I gulped.

"Walk in front of me," he ordered.

He nudged me through the door. Then he led me to a gate in the barbed-wire fence.

How had I missed the gate? Some detective I was. I couldn't even find a gate in a fence. I started to feel really sad and scared.

"Where are we going?" I quietly asked Wolf.

"We're going to my house," he said angrily. "My old man will be home any minute. He'll decide what we should do with a dirty, rotten burglar."

"Burglar?" I said, choking on the word.

"What else do you call breaking and entering?" Wolf said. Then he pushed me forward. I had no choice but to walk toward the Mueller cabin. I couldn't outrun Wolf.

Wolf slid open the bolt on the cabin door and pushed me inside. We entered a cluttered room that looked like it was used for everything from cooking to sleeping. It smelled like bacon grease and old socks.

In one corner, boxes were stacked from the floor to the ceiling. Each box had a mailing label on it.

"Is that the peridot you stole from the reservation?" I said, pointing toward the boxes.

Wolf seemed startled. "Shut up," he replied. "Just sit in that chair and shut up." He pushed me toward a rickety old chair in one corner of the room.

I did what he said. I mean, what was I supposed to do? I was scared he'd hurt me if I didn't listen to him.

Wolf went outside. I could hear him walking around, kicking branches.

I hoped that his dad wouldn't come back. Wolf was bigger than me, but Luther was really scary. I didn't know what I'd do if he showed up.

A few minutes later, Wolf came back into the cabin. "You really should mind your own business," he said.

He reached down and grabbed my arms. He squeezed them as he pulled me up from the chair. "I was going to tie you up, but I have a better idea," he said, pushing me toward the door.

I was beginning to hope he was going to let me go. But I didn't really think he would. That didn't seem like the kind of thing Wolf would do.

Wolf didn't say a word as he led me down the trail, which I knew led to the shed by the creek. If I walked too slowly, he pushed me to keep me moving.

It started to thunder. Big splashy raindrops were beginning to fall. Wolf started walking faster and faster.

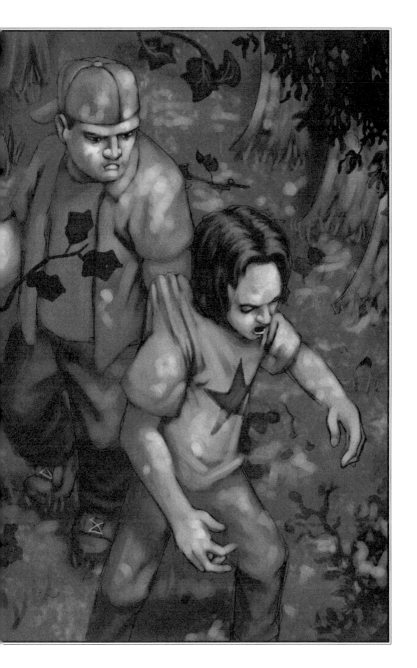

When we reached the shed, Wolf turned his back on me long enough to prop open the door.

In that split second, I dug into my pocket. I pulled my lizard keychain out and dropped it in the brush by the cabin.

I figured if Mr. Barker came looking for me, he might see it. It was my only chance.

Inside the shed, Wolf moved the rowboat. He opened the trap door.

Then he picked me up and stuffed me down inside, like I was a letter he was dropping into a mailbox.

I fell a short distance until my feet hit what felt like a hard dirt floor. Before I could put up my hands, the door above me shut.

I heard a bolt slide. Then I heard a scraping sound. Wolf was moving the rowboat back in place.

For a long time, I didn't try to move. I just stood in the darkness, listening to the silence.

No one was there to hear me scream. Not even my little lizard keychain.

[CHAPTER 10]

UNDERGROUND

After I yelled for a while, my throat started to hurt. I knew I was wasting my time screaming, since no one could hear me. So I decided to explore the hole where Wolf Mueller had put me.

I didn't have much room to move around. I reached into my pocket and took out my flashlight.

I could tell the battery was weak, but it gave off enough light to show me that there were dirt walls all around me.

The area I was in was pretty small. There was also a tiny room to my left. It was about the size of a bathroom. I decided to check it out.

I had to duck to get into the room. When I shone my light inside, I saw that I was not alone. A one-legged skeleton with a tuft of black hair on its skull lay in a heap in the corner.

I'd found the runaway skeleton.

When my knees stopped shaking, I explored the rest of my prison. There were lots of crates and boxes. None of them seemed to hold any food.

I realized that I was starving. I wished I had my bag, with the lunch Mrs. Barker had made.

"I can't think about food right now," I said out loud.

The skeleton glared back at me.

"What do you care?" I said. "Your eating days are over."

And so are yours, unless you find a way out of this place, I told myself.

I slumped down on one of the wooden crates and shut off the flickering flashlight. I needed to think.

I knew there was no way to open the trap door. Even if there was, I would never be able to move the rowboat away from it to get out. That left me two choices. I could dig my way out, or I could die.

I decided to dig.

My nickname, Topo, means "mole." Dad called me that when I was a little kid, because I liked digging in the dirt. I would sit in our backyard for hours, digging.

Moles have sharp claws, which help them scrape through dirt. They spend most of their lives underground.

But I didn't want to be a real mole. I couldn't wait to get back to the sunlight and fresh air. And all I had to dig with was my pocketknife.

The ceiling was made of rotting wood beams and boards. I stuck my knife between two of the ceiling boards.

The blade came back covered in dirt. That meant that part of the room I was in was actually under the dirt outside the shed.

Now I needed a plan. I turned off the flashlight. It was completely black in the room.

I remembered reading a story in school. It was about a blind man. He was the only person who survived a horrible plane crash.

Using his hands and his ears, the blind man managed to find his way down a mountain and get help.

If he could do that, I can do this, I told myself.

I decided to stand in the place where Wolf had dropped me. I knew it was directly under the trap door and the shed.

From there, I could begin removing the ceiling boards from my prison. That way, if some dirt started pouring in, I wouldn't be buried beneath it.

I turned the flashlight back on, but it flickered as I started working. I figured I had about fifteen minutes left before it would go out altogether.

Because the ceiling boards were rotten, they easily chipped away when I stabbed them with my knife.

Each board was about a foot wide. If I removed two, I would have room to start digging up. There was about a foot of dirt on top of the ceiling, I guessed. Most of it would fall into the room when I got a board out.

CRACK!

The end of one board fell into the room. So did a shower of dirt and rocks. It buried part of the skeleton.

"Sorry, mister," I said.

I stretched out my arm into the space where the board had been. I'd hoped my hand would break through into the outside air. But it touched more dirt. I had no way of knowing how far underground I was.

The second board was harder to loosen. My arms hurt from the effort. Finally, after about ten minutes, a tiny piece of the board broke free. But the rest stayed firmly in place.

Then, with a final flicker, my flashlight went out.

I was wrapped in darkness.

I carefully felt my way to a wooden crate and sat down. Lots of stuff went through my mind.

I thought about Mono and wondered how he'd get along without me. He was a tough little guy. And he was pretty smart. I decided that he would be able to make his way through life on his own.

Would the Barkers keep my little brother? They didn't have kids of their own and they seemed to enjoy having me and Mono there. But would they keep him if I wasn't around to take care of him?

They both worked. The only reason they'd agreed to take us for the summer was that I could watch Mono during the day.

I could only hope that Mono would work his charm on them. He could be pretty lovable if he tried.

Then I thought about my parents. When they'd first disappeared, I couldn't sleep at night. I was scared and angry.

Had they left us on purpose? Deep down, I didn't believe that. Now, in the dark, I could picture Dad's jolly face and long mustache. I could smell Mom's lilac scent and hear her merry laugh.

Were they still alive? If so, could they sense that one of their sons was in big trouble?

As I sat in my underground prison, I promised myself one thing.

If, somehow, I was rescued, I would try to find Mom and Dad. Maybe Miss Phinney, the librarian, could help me search for them on the computer.

SCREECH!

The noise came from over my head. Then I heard a thump.

I knew what those noises were. Someone was moving the rowboat off the trap door.

My heart thudded. I held my breath. I might be able to fight off Wolf. It was worth a try. I ducked and backed into the little room. Then I took out my knife, pulled out the blade, and waited.

Slowly, the trap door opened.

CHAPTER 11

LUCKY LIZARD

"Topo! Topo, are you in there?"

Mono? Was I dreaming, or was that really Mono's voice?

"Topo?" called a man's voice. "Topo?"

It was Mr. Barker! I scrambled out of the dirt room and into the light.

"It's him, it's him!" Mono shrieked.

The noise of his shoes tapping above me told me he was doing his Mono dance.

"Topo! You're all right!" Mr. Barker said, his voice shaky.

Soon his strong arms lifted me out. I stood trembling on the shed floor.

When my eyes got used to the light, I saw two other men. I recognized one as the county sheriff, Sheriff Petrie.

The other man stepped forward and shook my hand. "Nice to meet you, Topo," he said. "I'm Deputy Martinez."

Deputy Martinez was wearing a raincoat, and water dripped off it onto the floor, making a small puddle on the wooden floorboards.

A loud clap of thunder shook the shed. To me, it was the most beautiful sound in the world.

I had thought I would never hear thunder again. I felt like crying.

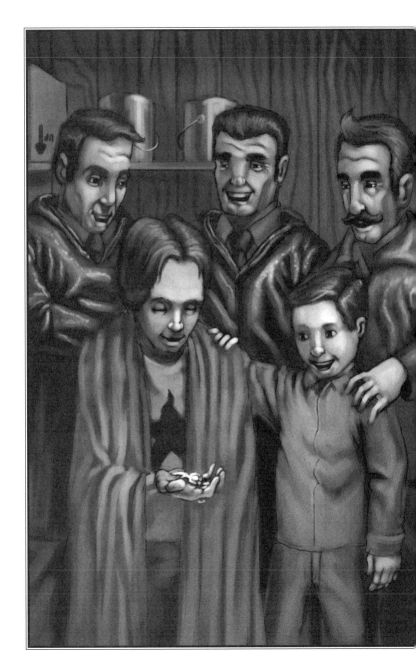

Mono reached up and put something in my hand. My lizard keychain!

"I found the clue, Topo," Mono said. "You dropped it, just like in Hansel and Gretel when they made a breadcrumb trail."

"That's right," Mr. Barker said. "Your brother found that and knew it was yours."

"I'm a good detective, aren't I?" Mono asked, smiling proudly.

I could only nod. I felt too shaky to do anything else.

Mr. Barker put his arm around me. "You certainly are, Mono," he told my brother. "But now let's get Topo home. We'll have plenty of time to talk later."

He handed me a blanket to wrap around myself. The rain had chilled the normally warm air.

We dashed to the sheriff's car, which sat outside the shed. We all piled inside and headed to the Barkers' house.

Mrs. Barker raced out to greet us. She was laughing and crying at the same time. She immediately led us all to the kitchen.

Soon I was sipping a steaming cup of soup. After a few minutes, I started to feel better, more like myself. Then I just felt tired. My eyes started to close.

Mrs. Barker looked at me and said, "I think Topo needs to get some sleep now, everyone. Let's take a break from this party and let him get to bed."

"We'll need to talk to you tomorrow, just to tie up some loose ends," Sheriff Petrie said as he left.

"I'll bring him by in the morning," Mr. Barker said.

Sheriff Petrie smiled. "You're a smart young man, Topo," he said. "Maybe in a few years you'll decide to come work for us."

Then he looked at Mono. "You too, Mono," Sheriff Petrie said. "We'll need another detective once you're old enough."

I had a gazillion questions I wanted to ask, but the soup and warm blanket were making me tired. Mr. Barker helped me walk to my bed. I must have fallen asleep as soon as my head hit the pillow.

The next thing I knew, the sun woke me. Mono was dressed and sitting on the edge of his bed. He was staring at me. When he saw that I was awake, he got a huge smile on his face.

"Mrs. Barker said I shouldn't wake you up. I didn't, right?" Mono asked. "I didn't bug you. You just woke up by yourself."

I blinked, feeling confused. It took me a while to realize that everything that had happened was not a dream.

As I got dressed in jeans and a T-shirt, Mono told me everything that I'd missed the day before.

An hour or so after they left, it had started storming. Mono and Mr. Barker had come home from the dig early.

When I wasn't there, they were a little bit worried, but they figured I was just fishing. Mono had a feeling that something else was going on, but he didn't say anything to Mr. Barker.

Mr. Barker said that he thought I'd be okay. He told Mono that I knew how to handle myself in the outdoors. He said I would find shelter from the storm and come home after it had passed.

Then he noticed that I hadn't taken my fishing rod.

"Don't get mad, Topo," Mono said now. "I was so scared something happened to you. I told Mr. Barker everything about the skeleton. I got your notebook and gave it to him. He read all the stuff you wrote in it. Then he called the sheriff."

"I'm not mad, Mono," I said. "You saved my life, man."

Mono did his monkey dance again.

CHAPTER 12

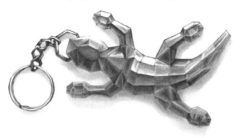

A GREAT TEAM

At the breakfast table, Mr. Barker told me more. As soon as he had finished reading the notes in my notebook, he and Mono got into the car.

They'd gone to the Muellers' cabin first. They got there just as Luther and Wolf Mueller were backing down the driveway in their pickup with a load of peridot.

It turned out I was right about the peridot. The Muellers were mailing it to buyers in other states.

I was right about the skeleton, too. Luther had dug it up by accident while he was illegally on Apache land. The police were looking for him.

"I think Wolf was just doing what his father taught him to do," Mr. Barker added. "So after he tells the police what he knows, he probably won't go to prison."

Despite what Wolf had done to me, I felt glad that he wasn't going to jail. I couldn't imagine having a father like Luther Mueller. I felt really sorry for Wolf.

When we finished eating, Mr. Barker and I headed to town and the sheriff's office.

On the way, he told me that he and Mrs. Barker wanted to keep Mono and me, if we agreed to stay.

We parked in front of the sheriff's office. Mr. Barker put his hand on my shoulder.

"We're not trying to replace your parents, Topo," he told me. "In fact, if you'd like, I can help you try to find out what happened to them. I think we'd make a good team."

"I'd like that," I said. "Of course, my number-one detective helper is Mono."

Mr. Barker laughed. "He's a great helper!" he said.

I gave Mr. Barker a hug. "Thanks for everything, George," I said shyly. Then I slipped a hand in my jeans pocket.

My lizard keychain was there. Like the first time I touched him, I knew that everything would work out all right.

ABOUT THE AUTHOR

Kathleen Muldoon teaches writing for the Institute of Children's Literature. She is also a freelance writer and has authored thirteen books and dozens of magazine articles and stories for children. Her main focus is writing books for the educational market. When not writing, she enjoys playing with her cat, Prissy, and her parakeet, Abraham.

ABOUT THE ILLUSTRATOR

Phillip Hilliker lives most of his life in the strange and creepy realm in his head. As such, becoming an illustrator was pretty much the only career path that would allow him to stay there. Phil graduated from the College for Creative Studies and has spent the majority of the past few years illustrating various role-playing-game books. He lives in Arizona with his awesome scientist of a wife and their imaginary pet bunny, Balthazar.

GLOSSARY

abandoned (uh-BAN-duhnd)—no longer used

archaeologist (ar-kee-OL-uh-jist)—someone who studies the past by digging up old buildings and objects and studying them

burial grounds (BER-ee-uhl groundz)—places where bodies were buried

evidence (EV-uh-duhnss)—information and facts that help prove something

foster (FOSS-tur)—foster parents look after children who are not their own

hunch (HUHNCH)—an unproven idea

illegal (i-LEE-guhl)—against the law

loco (LOH-koh)—the Spanish word for "crazy"

reservation (rez-ur-VAY-shuhn)—an area of land set aside by the government for a specific purpose

sacred (SAY-krid)—very important and deserving great respect

skeleton (SKEL-uh-tuhn)—the framework of bones that supports and protects the body

DISCUSSION QUESTIONS

1. Did Topo do the right thing when he went to the Muellers' land alone? Why or why not?

2. Can you think of any other ways Topo could have tried to get information about the skeleton?

3. Why were the Muellers stealing the peridot?

WRITING PROMPTS

1. Sometimes it can be interesting to think about a story from another person's point of view. Try writing chapter 11 from Mono's point of view. What does Topo's little brother see and hear? What does he think about? How does he feel?

2. Topo and Mono both have nicknames that are Spanish words for animals. What is your nickname? How did you get it? If you don't have a nickname, what nickname would you like to have? Why?

3. The special food that Topo and Mono eat on the reservation is acorn stew. If you were going to serve a special food to someone, what would it be? Why?

MORE ABOUT NATIVE AMERICANS

The Apaches (uh-PAH-cheez) are one of the best-known groups of Native Americans in America.

The Apaches originally lived in parts of Mexico and the southwestern United States, in what is now Arizona, New Mexico, and Texas.

Apache art included fine beadwork and basketry. The Apaches traded with other nearby tribes.

Today, there are as many as 6,000 Apaches in Arizona, Oklahoma, and New Mexico. Some of those people live on reservations.

Years ago, land was taken from the Native Americans when they fought with the expanding United States.

AND RESERVATIONS

Afterward, the U.S. gave a small amount of the land back. Those small portions of land are now known as reservations. Some Native Americans still live on reservations.

Though the reservations are part of the United States, some reservations are independent nations called sovereign (SOV-ur-in) nations.

These nations make their own laws. They may have different rules than neighboring cities and towns.

Even though a Native American kid may live on a reservation, his or her life is just like any other American kid's life.

STARCUPS!, *the Harrison Ford High School musical, is in danger. Everyone's a suspect. Kyle Sutton and his only friend, Mindy, have to work together to catch the crook. The show must go on!*

You'll Love . . .

Steve Brezenoff

I DARE you

I DARE you!
by Steve Brezenoff

STONE ARCH *Mystery*

Gutter, Tad, Kayla, and May take turns giving each other dares. This time, Kayla is dared to sleep inside a creepy old house. The next morning, Kayla won't wake up. She's in a coma. Her friends will have to find out what happened.

INTERNET SITES

Do you want to know more about subjects related to this book? Or are you interested in learning about other topics? Then check out FactHound, a fun, easy way to find Internet sites.

Our investigative staff has already sniffed out great sites for you!

Here's how to use FactHound:

1. Visit *www.facthound.com*

2. Select your grade level.

3. To learn more about subjects related to this book, type in the book's ISBN number: **9781434208002**.

4. Click the **Fetch It** button.

FactHound will fetch the best Internet sites for you!